FRANKLYn

No Ordinary Fox

Dedicated to Benjamin, Samson & Eleanor.

This Book Belongs to:

....

Franklyn is no ordinary fox. The foxes you see in your town may be sly and cunning, but Franklyn is kind and caring. He's kind to squirrels, he's kind to rabbits, he's even kind to bugs and slugs.

You may see foxes tipping over people's bins and eating leftovers. Franklyn, however, prefers to eat the juicy berries and tasty nuts he finds scattered under trees and bushes.

Because Franklyn is so different, other foxes don't understand him at first. Foxes like Mitchell. Mitchell always used to bully Franklyn. In fact, Mitchell bullied all the other foxes.

'Hey, Franklyn! Why are you eating that carrot? You're a fox, not a rabbit! Hahaha!'

'Hey, Franklyn! Why are you talking to that robin? You should be EATING it! Hahaha!'

The other foxes would laugh along at Mitchell's mean jokes, mainly because they were scared of him.

However, there was one fox who didn't laugh. Her name was Florence. Secretly, she was rather fond of Franklyn. But she was too shy to tell him.

One day, Franklyn was sitting under a tree, playing with a cute little caterpillar. Suddenly, Mitchell jumped out at him from behind a bush.

Poor Franklyn shrieked with shock. They were quickly joined by some other foxes who had heard Franklyn scream. They wanted to see what was happening.

'What do we have here?' said Mitchell. 'I hope you're going to eat that stupid bug?'
'No,' replied Franklyn.
'Why not?' snarled the bushy-tailed bully. 'You're a fox! Foxes are meant to eat bugs. Bugs eat food out of the bins – OUR food! So why are you being nice to it?'
Franklyn ignored him.

'If you care more about bugs than foxes,' Mitchell sneered, 'why don't you just leave – and take your silly bug with you!' The other foxes mumbled in agreement.

Franklyn glanced at the little crowd. He noticed Florence standing there with them. She looked sad. Franklyn gave her a friendly smile and trotted off into the distance.

Florence felt a tight knot in her chest as she watched him go.

Was this the last time she'd see Franklyn Fox?

Mitchell was up to no good as usual. He was trying to sneak into someone's garden, but he couldn't get in. The people who lived there had put up a new, higher fence to keep foxes like Mitchell out.

Hi, Mitchell!

said a familiar, friendly voice.

Mitchell turned round. In front of him stood Franklyn holding a potted plant. 'What are you doing here? I thought I told you to leave!' growled the mean fox.

Oh, I'm just passing through!

Franklyn said.

Mitchell grunted and looked at the plant. 'What's the point of that?' he mocked.

But Mitchell didn't wait for an answer. He just shook his head and went back to trying to scale the fence. Franklyn went on his way. He left the plant outside Florence's home with a note that said 'From Franklyn'.

After another few weeks, Franklyn returned once more. This time, Mitchell was trying to steal from a dustbin. It was proving difficult. All the bins in the town had been replaced with new ones. These new bins were specially designed to stop animals from getting into them.

As Mitchell gnawed at the bin lid, trying to find a way to shove his face inside, he heard a familiar voice again.
'Hello, Mitchell,' said Franklyn. 'How are you?'
'What are you doing back here?' Mitchell growled.

Just passing through!

Franklyn said with a smile.

Luckily, Mitchell was so determined to get into the bin that he didn't pay much attention to Franklyn. Nor did he see that Franklyn was holding his friend, the caterpillar, on his paw. Which was just as well.

Franklyn went on his way. Once again, he headed for Florence's house. When he reached it this time, Florence was standing outside. 'Franklyn! How lovely to see you!' she cried. 'Thanks for the plant – it's started to grow tiny flower buds.'

'You're welcome, Florence,' Franklyn replied. 'I have another gift for you today.' And he handed her the caterpillar.

'Aw, he's sweet,' said Florence. 'Thank you, Franklyn! I'll hopefully see you again soon.'
And she waved as Franklyn disappeared once again.

A few weeks later, Franklyn passed through a third time. As he walked along singing to himself, he heard voices arguing. He walked on a bit further ... and came across Mitchell and another fox. They were fighting over scraps in the street.

Both foxes stopped arguing for a moment to look at him. Mitchell pointed at him and scoffed, 'Haha! Look, he's got a basket of berries. That stupid fox.'

The other fox laughed. Then he and Mitchell started arguing again. Franklyn strolled on, happy and carefree.

When Florence saw him, she ran over to him excitedly. 'Franklyn! I've got something to show you!' She held out the plant Franklyn had given her. There was a chrysalis hanging under one of the leaves.

As they looked at it, the chrysalis started to twitch. Then a beautiful butterfly emerged! It flicked its wings, rose into the air and fluttered around their heads.

Franklyn smiled and handed Florence the basket. 'These berries are for you too,' he said. 'Now, would you like to come and see where I live these days?'
'Yes, please!' Florence said gleefully.
'Follow me, then,' Franklyn replied. 'I'll carry the plant.' And they set off through the town.

They saw Mitchell. The argument he'd been having had turned into a proper fight, and the two angry foxes were now rolling around together on the ground. Franklyn and Florence said nothing. They slid past and headed to the countryside.

The sun shone down on them, and they shared the basket of delicious berries as they went. When they reached a stone wall, Franklyn said, 'Through here.' And he squeezed into a hole.

Florence followed him. As she came out the other side, she couldn't believe her eyes. They were standing in a field. It was full of rows of tiny trees and shrubs. 'This is it!' Franklyn said.

'You live here?' Florence replied. She looked shocked.
'Sort of,' Franklyn answered. 'My home is this way.'

Florence followed him through another hole, this time in the ground.

Not for the first time that day, she shrieked with excitement. She found herself in a huge underground house. There were tunnels and rooms everywhere. 'Wow!' cried Florence. 'This is amazing! You did all this yourself?'

'Not quite.' Franklyn shook his head. 'I had help from the local rabbits. I promised them I'd return the favour by feeding them. All the trees and shrubs you saw outside have grown from seeds I planted.' Franklyn showed Florence the view from his window.

'You see, instead of us all trying to survive on scraps from bins, we can eat fresh fruit. Then we can put the leftover seeds in the earth to grow more trees.'
Florence smiled from ear to ear.
'Do you like it?' Franklyn asked.

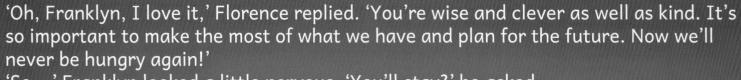

'Oh, Franklyn, I love it,' Florence replied. 'You're wise and clever as well as kind. It's so important to make the most of what we have and plan for the future. Now we'll never be hungry again!'
'So ...' Franklyn looked a little nervous. 'You'll stay?' he asked.

'You bet!' Florence replied. 'I want to stay and help you grow more things – starting right now! Where shall we plant this beautiful flower?'

Franklyn Financial Management created this book to help educate young children about the benefits of investing in their future.

The three questions below will help you to start a discussion about the topic:

1. What are the differences between Franklyn and Mitchell?

2. Why is it important to plant seeds?

3. Can you think of other ways of saving for the future?

Printed in the UK by NMC Design+Print, a social enterprise forming part of the NeuroMuscular Centre in Winsford, Cheshire, UK: nmcentre.com

Copyright belongs to Franklyn Financial Management
Story written by Nick Jones: www.nickjonesauthor.co.uk
Illustrated by Ant Harding: www.antharding.co.uk
Published by Franklyn Financial Management: www.franklynfm.co.uk

For more books by Nick Jones visit:
www.full-media.co.uk

For more books by Ant Harding visit:
www.okichobee.co.uk